To my dear Filiberto, my storytelling prince.
You have always been and will always be a part of this story.

Alicia Acosta

To Miguel, for his considerable help. A thousand thanks.
To Luis A., for his patience and support.

Cecilia Moreno

The Incredible Ship of Captain Skip
Somos8 Series

© Text: Alicia Acosta, 2020
© Illustrations: Cecilia Moreno, 2020
© Edition: NubeOcho, 2020
© Translation: Cecilia Ross, 2020
www.nubeocho.com · hello@nubeocho.com

Original title: *El increíble barco del capitán Marco*
Text editing: Rima Noureddine, Rebecca Packard, Caroline Dookie

Adapted from a traditional oral tale.

First edition: May 2021
ISBN: 978-84-18133-16-9
Legal Deposit: M-8851-2020

Printed in Portugal.

THE INCREDIBLE SHIP
OF CAPTAIN SKIP

Alicia Acosta   Cecilia Moreno

nubeOCHO

Skip used to live in the desert, but she was tired of all the **dust and sand**. One day, she decided to leave home in search of adventure on the **Seven Seas**.

But before embarking on her journey, Skip needed **a ship**. She found an old vessel with **a mast so high** it nearly touched **the sky**.

Skip put on her **white captain's shirt.**
Now she had her ship, but there was still
something missing...

"I need a **crew!**
Will you join me on this voyage?"

Skip and her crew worked hard to prepare for their **perilous adventure**.

Finally, the incredible ship of Captain Skip was ready to sail.

WEIGH ANCHOR!

Captain Skip and her crew began their journey. They traveled far until they reached the **Yellow Sea,** near China. The waters there were very beautiful, but they were known to be treacherous.

As they threaded their way through the islands, an enormous tidal wave dashed the ship against some rocks and **cracked the stern.**

Brave Captain Skip examined **the damage** and decided that the ship was still seaworthy.

"Shall we press on?" she asked.

The incredible ship of Captain Skip unfurled its sails, and they set off again. They sailed past the **islands of Japan** until they reached the **Sulu Sea.**

This is a sea near the **Philippines,** known for its rough and dangerous waters.

Suddenly, **the tentacles of a giant octopus** rose from beneath the waves and tried to sink the ship.

Captain Skip held fast to the **helm,** and they sailed away as quickly as they could.

The incredible ship of Captain Skip managed to escape, but the octopus's strong tentacles had snapped **the prow** clean off.

Fearless Captain Skip examined the damage and made what repairs she could. She decided that the ship was still **seaworthy.**

"Shall we press on?" she asked.

Tear off the front part of your paper ship.

Once more, the incredible ship of Captain Skip **sailed on**...

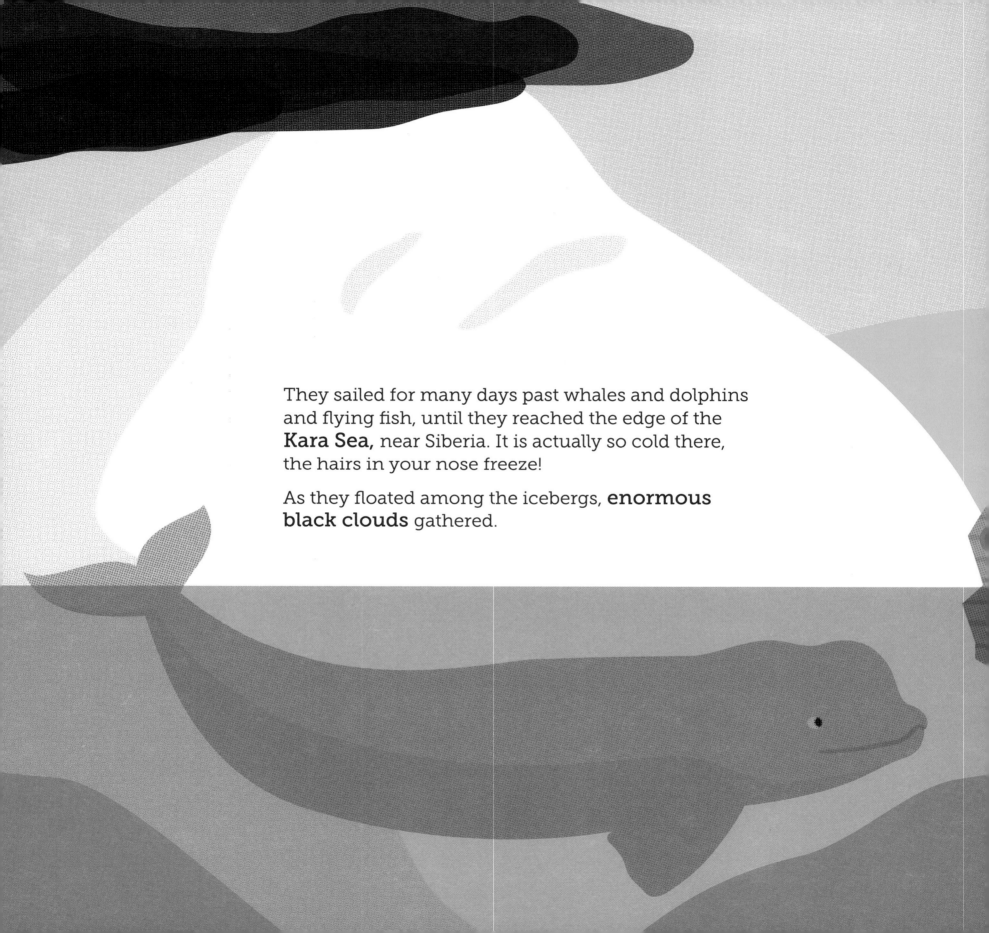

They sailed for many days past whales and dolphins and flying fish, until they reached the edge of the **Kara Sea,** near Siberia. It is actually so cold there, the hairs in your nose freeze!

As they floated among the icebergs, **enormous black clouds** gathered.

"Storm!" cried Captain Skip.

Heavy rain began to fall, and suddenly a powerful **bolt of lightning** hit the mast of Captain Skip's incredible ship... and split it **right down the middle!**

Tear off the top part of your paper ship.

Captain Skip knew, just as everyone does,
that a ship cannot sail without a **mast**. With
a heart full of sadness, she yelled,

ABANDON SHIP!

Captain Skip and her crew were safe **on the lifeboats,** but their incredible ship sank to the bottom of the sea...

GLUB, GLUB, GLUB, GLUB

Years passed, and rumors began to spread in portside taverns. **Sailors and pirates** shared the legend of a great treasure hidden inside Captain Skip's incredible ship, one that would make whoever found it very rich.

Many set out in search of **this treasure**.

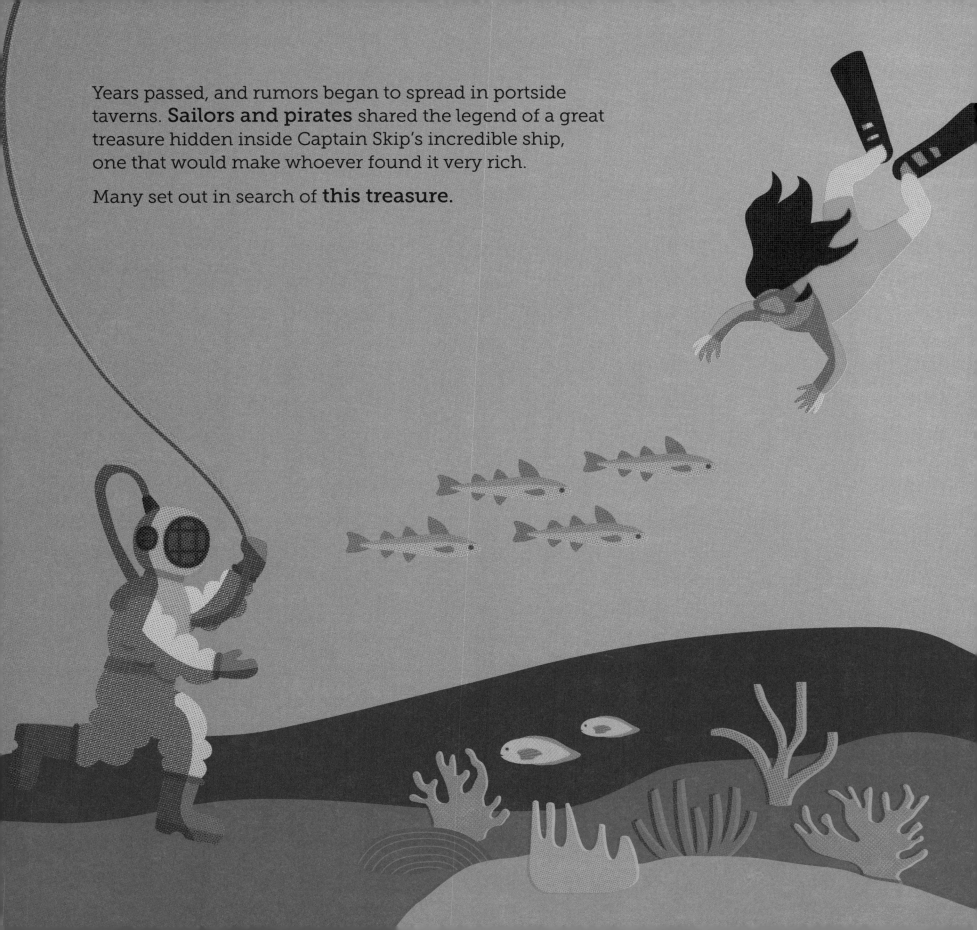

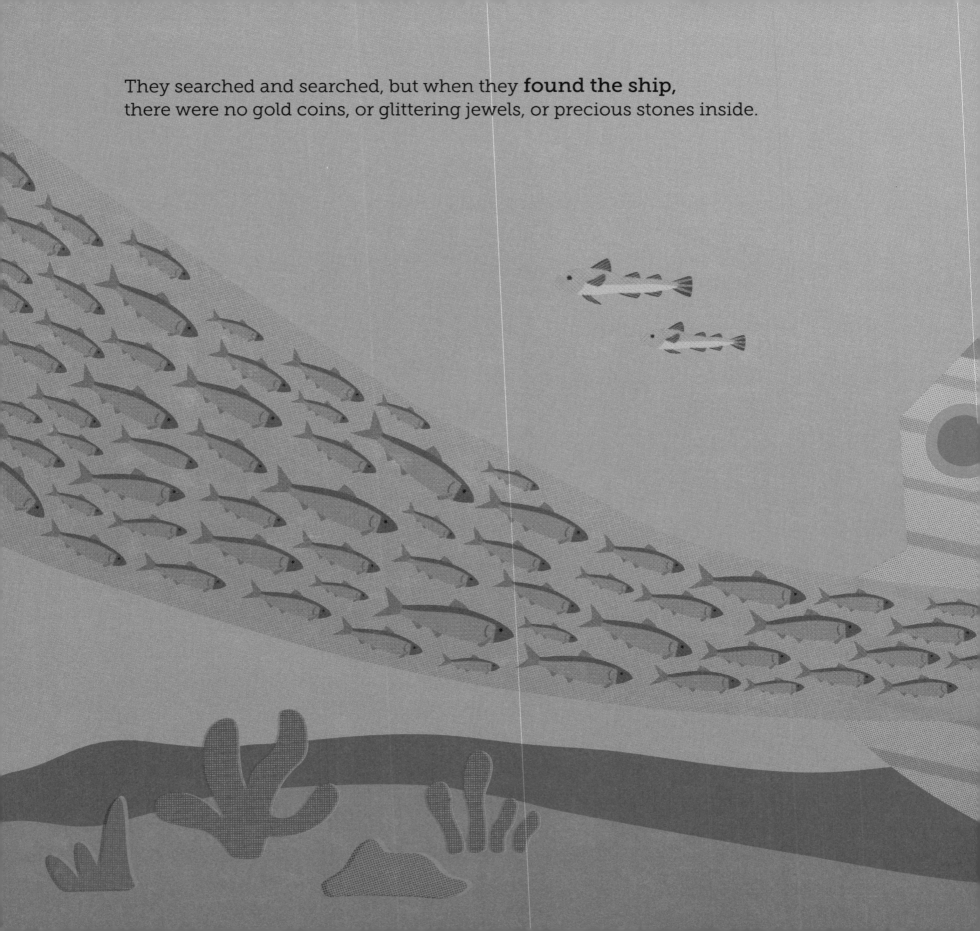

They searched and searched, but when they **found the ship,**
there were no gold coins, or glittering jewels, or precious stones inside.

Instead, they discovered **a different kind of treasure**.
For inside the ship they came upon...

THE WHITE SHIRT OF CAPTAIN SKIP!